AFTER 5

She Comes Home Different

A Novel

Avenyx Rae

ISBN: 979-8-9958645-0-9

Published by Rae Publishing

Printed in the United States of America

Acknowledgements

This book was shaped by the voices, perspectives, and honest reflections of those who took the time to read, question, and challenge its depth.

Thank you to those who saw pieces of themselves in Imani and offered insight that strengthened her story.

Your feedback didn't just refine the pages – it gave them dimensions.

For the woman who built everything—

and still chose herself.

CHAPTER 1

Control wasn't something Imani learned.

It was something she built—layer by layer, decision by decision—until it

became inseparable from how she moved through the world.

Imani didn't build a company. She built systems that organizations depended on to function.

It showed up in everything.

In the way she spoke—measured, never rushed.

In the way she paused before responding, letting silence do part of the work
for her.

Even in the way people adjusted when she entered a room.

Most of them didn't realize they were doing it.

She always did.

Her office sat high above the city, far enough that the noise softened before

it reached her windows. Floor-to-ceiling glass framed a skyline that never

really stopped moving, but inside, everything felt contained.

Intentional.

Clean.

Nothing unnecessary.

She liked it that way.

It wasn't just preference.

It was protection.

Because control meant nothing had the chance to fall apart where she could see it.

"Your ten o'clock is here."

Marisol didn't step all the way inside when she opened the door. She never

did. It was one of those small consistencies Imani appreciated without ever

commenting on.

Imani finished the paragraph she was reading before looking up.

"Send him in."

The man who walked in didn't hesitate.

That stood out immediately.

Most people slowed down, even if it was subtle. Something about the

room—about her—shifted their pace without them realizing it.

He didn't adjust at all.

"Imani."

No title.

No hesitation.

Just her name.

She let that sit for a second—not long enough to feel intentional, but long

enough to register.

"You're early."

He gave a slight shrug, like it wasn't worth explaining.

"Didn't see a reason to wait."

He didn't try to fill the silence after that.

Didn't glance around the room.

Didn't shift in his seat.

Didn't attempt to read her.

He just… stayed where he was.

Imani leaned back slightly, studying him in a way that didn't look like she was

studying him.

That was new.

"Sit," she said.

He already had.

That almost made her smile.

Almost.

She folded her hands lightly on the desk.

"Let's be clear about why you're here."

A faint shift crossed his expression. Not quite amusement, not quite

challenge.

"I already am."

Imani held his gaze.

There was no push behind his words.

No attempt to impress.

No visible effort to position himself.

Just certainty.

And that—more than anything else—caught her attention.

Because certainty without performance was rare.

She had seen confidence before.

She had seen arrogance, hesitation, and overcompensation.

This wasn't any of those.

It was quieter.

Steadier.

And for the first time in a while, something inside her shifted—not enough

to disrupt her control, but enough to make her aware of it.

This conversation wasn't going to move the way most did.

And she wasn't entirely sure yet if that was an advantage—

or something she needed to watch more closely.

But she knew one thing.

She wasn't going to look away from it.

CHAPTER 2

Imani didn't rush conversations.

She didn't need to.

People revealed more than they intended when they were given space—

especially the kind of space that wasn't filled for them.

Silence had a way of doing that.

Most people tried to escape it.

They filled it with explanations, clarifications, unnecessary detail—anything

to regain authority of the moment.

Imani let them.

It told her everything she needed to know.

Malik didn't move that way.

He didn't rush to speak after her question. Didn't lean forward, didn't adjust

his tone, didn't search for the version of the answer that would land best.

He considered it.

Then answered.

"The pressure," he said. "And what matters."

Imani watched him for a moment longer than usual.

"That's not the same as being prepared."

He nodded once.

"No. It's not."

No defensiveness.

No attempt to reframe it.

Just acknowledgment.

That was… unusual.

Most people corrected themselves when they realized they hadn't given a

"complete" answer.

They expanded. Justified. Tried to close whatever gap they thought existed.

Malik didn't.

He let the statement stand.

Imani leaned forward slightly, shifting the tone without making it obvious.

"And that doesn't concern you?"

Another pause.

Not hesitation.

Consideration.

"It tells me what to focus on," he said.

That answer was more precise.

Not broader.

Not safer.

More intentional.

Imani held his gaze.

"And what exactly are you focusing on?"

He didn't answer immediately this time.

Not because he didn't know.

Because he was choosing how much to say.

"The parts that actually change the outcome," he said finally.

There it was again.

Not performance.

Structure.

Imani sat back slightly.

Most people talked around impact.

They described effort. Process. Contribution.

He went straight to outcome.

That mattered.

"Confidence doesn't guarantee performance," she said.

Malik nodded.

"I know."

A brief pause settled between them.

"But hesitation guarantees failure," he added.

Imani didn't respond right away.

Not because she disagreed.

Because the statement didn't feel like something he rehearsed.

It felt like something he had already learned.

And that—more than anything else—shifted her assessment.

He wasn't trying to prove he belonged in the room.

He was already operating like he did.

Imani let the silence settle one more time before closing the conversation.

"Alright," she said.

A small shift in tone.

"Let's see how that translates when it matters."

Malik didn't respond.

But something in the way he held her gaze changed.

Not tension.

Focus.

And just like that—

the conversation moved forward.

But something else moved with it.

Something she hadn't defined yet.

And for now—

she didn't try to.

That should have been the end of it.

But it wasn't.

And she couldn't explain why.

CHAPTER 3

By the time Malik left her office, Imani didn't reach for the next task

immediately.

That, on its own, was unusual.

Her schedule didn't allow for pauses that weren't intentional.

And she rarely made space for them.

But this time—

she did.

She stood by the window, one hand resting lightly against the glass, her

reflection faint against the city moving below.

Everything outside continued exactly as expected.

Predictable.

Constant.

Inside—

her thoughts weren't as structured.

The conversation hadn't followed her rhythm.

That was new.

And she didn't like not immediately understanding why.

The conversation hadn't followed her rhythm.

That was the first thing she noted.

She had guided it—subtly at first, then more directly.

Tested tone.

Adjusted pacing.

Created space where she expected response.

It hadn't moved the way most conversations did.

Not resistant.

Controlled.

That distinction mattered.

"Thoughts?"

Marisol's voice broke the quiet, just before the door closed behind her.

Imani didn't turn immediately.

"Too early to decide."

Marisol stepped further into the room this time, studying her in a way most

people didn't attempt.

"That's not how you usually operate."

Imani glanced over her shoulder.

"No," she said evenly. "It's not."

A brief silence passed.

"You're considering him," Marisol said.

Not a question.

Imani walked back toward her desk, slower than her usual pace.

"I'm evaluating him."

Marisol's expression didn't change, but her tone shifted slightly.

"There's a difference."

Imani paused just enough to acknowledge it.

"I'm aware."

She picked up the file again, flipping it open without fully focusing on the

contents.

Her attention wasn't there.

"He doesn't overcompensate," she said after a moment.

Marisol tilted her head slightly.

"That's what stood out to you?"

Imani looked up.

"Yes."

Because most people did.

They filled gaps.

Pushed too hard.

Spoke too much.

Tried to establish presence instead of simply having it.

"He also doesn't rush," she added.

Marisol leaned lightly against the desk.

"That can go either way."

Imani nodded once.

"I know."

Another pause.

"And?" Marisol pressed.

Imani closed the file this time.

"He's intentional," she said.

A beat.

"And that's harder to teach."

The room settled into silence again.

But this time—

it didn't linger.

Because Imani had already decided what came next.

Not about Malik.

About the process.

"Set up the follow-up," she said.

Marisol straightened.

"You're moving forward."

Imani met her gaze.

"I'm giving him space to show me how he handles pressure."

Marisol's expression softened slightly.

"That usually answers everything."

Imani nodded.

"Yes," she said quietly.

"It does."

CHAPTER 4

The drive home took twenty-three minutes.

Twenty-three minutes of emails.

Three phone calls.

Two text messages.

And one problem that had already been solved before she reached the second traffic light.

Imani parked in the reserved space beneath her building and sat for a moment after turning off the engine.

Silence.

Rare.

Temporary.

But noticeable.

The lobby attendant greeted her by name.

She smiled politely.

The elevator carried her upward.

Thirty-four floors.

Thirty-four floors between the version of herself everyone knew and the version nobody ever saw.

The apartment door closed behind her.

And suddenly—

everything stopped.

No meetings.

No expectations.

No decisions.

No one waiting.

No one needing.

No one calling her name.

Imani placed her bag on the marble console near the entrance.

Keys in the tray.

Shoes aligned.

Jacket hung.

The routine never changed.

She moved through the apartment with practiced efficiency.

The living room looked exactly as it should.

The kitchen looked untouched.

The dining table sat perfectly arranged.

Six chairs.

Not one occupied.

A faint laugh escaped her.

Not because anything was funny.

Because she couldn't remember the last time she hosted dinner.

Or the last time anyone sat there long enough to leave a glass behind.

Her phone buzzed.

Another message.

Another request.

Another problem.

Imani looked at the screen.

Then set it face down.

That was unusual.

The room felt larger than it did in the morning.

Empty spaces often did.

She walked toward the windows.

The city stretched endlessly beneath her.

Lights.

Movement.

Life.

Everyone heading somewhere.

Everyone returning to someone.

For a moment she wondered what that felt like.

Not responsibility.

Not leadership.

Belonging.

The thought surprised her.

Enough that she immediately pushed it away.

She had worked too hard for this life.

Built too much.

Sacrificed too much.

Success had a cost.

She understood that.

The problem was—

lately she wasn't sure she remembered what she paid for it.

Her reflection stared back from the glass.

Confident.

Composed.

Respected.

Alone.

Imani looked away first.

CHAPTER 5

Pressure revealed things people didn't plan to show.

That's why Imani used it.

Not to break people—

but to understand them.

By midweek, Malik had been fully integrated into the pace of
the
organization.

No transition period.

No gradual adjustment.

He was placed directly into motion.

Deadlines didn't shift.

Expectations didn't lower.

And no one paused to make space for him to catch up.

Imani watched from a distance.

She didn't step in unnecessarily.

Didn't guide every move.

Because performance under instruction didn't tell her much.

What mattered was how someone moved when no one was
directing them.

At 11:22, she got her answer.

The meeting wasn't his.

But by the time it ended—

he had shaped it.

Not by dominating the room.

By clarifying it.

Imani stood just outside the glass wall, unnoticed.

Watching.

Voices overlapped.

Points circled.

Someone pushed a concern that didn't actually change anything.

Another tried to redirect but lacked precision.

Malik didn't interrupt.

He let it play out.

Tracked it.

Waited.

Then—

"Let's narrow this down to what actually changes the outcome."

The shift was immediate.

Not because he raised his voice.

Because he removed everything unnecessary.

Imani didn't move.

That was control.

Not force.

Clarity.

And clarity—

moved people faster than pressure ever could.

CHAPTER 6

Imani didn't give recognition lightly.

It wasn't about withholding.

It was about value.

If everything was acknowledged, nothing carried weight.

So when she noticed something—

it meant something.

By Thursday, Malik's presence had settled into the
environment in a way that

didn't require explanation.

It wasn't loud.

But it was noticeable.

People adjusted around him.

Not because he demanded it.

Because he didn't.

That was the part that stood out.

He didn't push for alignment.

He moved as if it was already expected.

And people responded to that.

Imani noticed it in the smallest ways.

Conversations shortened.

Decisions came faster.

Less unnecessary explanation.

It wasn't dominance.

It was efficiency.

And efficiency—

was power in its cleanest form.

At 2:03, she tested it.

Not obviously.

But intentionally.

A conversation that had already run too long.

Too many voices.

Too many directions.

Imani could have ended it immediately.

Instead—

she let it continue.

Watched.

Waited.

Malik didn't step in right away.

He let it unfold.

Then—

"Are we solving the problem, or just talking about it?"

The room went quiet.

Not because of the tone.

Because of the truth behind it.

Imani didn't hide her reaction this time.

It was subtle.

But it was there.

And Malik noticed.

Of course he did.

Later, when the room cleared, he stayed back.

Not lingering.

Intentional.

"You let that run longer than it needed to," he said.

Imani met his gaze.

"Yes."

A brief pause.

"You wanted to see what I would do."

She held his gaze.

"I wanted to see what you wouldn't do."

That landed.

Because the difference mattered.

He nodded once.

"And?"

Imani didn't answer immediately.

Because when something mattered—

she didn't rush it.

"You don't force control," she said.

Malik's expression remained steady.

"That's not always the best approach."

Imani leaned back slightly.

"No."

A brief pause.

"But it's the right one when it works."

Silence settled again.

Measured.

Balanced.

Then—

"You're not easy to read," Malik said.

Imani's expression shifted—just slightly.

"That's intentional."

He studied her for a moment.

Then nodded.

"I figured."

And just like that—

the moment ended.

But something stayed.

Not tension.

Recognition.

CHAPTER 7

Marisol rarely asked personal questions.

She understood boundaries.

She respected them.

Which was why Imani noticed immediately when she lingered after everyone else left.

"You ever regret it?"

Imani looked up from her laptop.

"Regret what?"

Marisol crossed her arms.

"The cost."

The question hung between them.

Imani knew exactly what she meant.

The company.

The success.

The years.

Everything.

She leaned back slowly.

"That's a broad question."

"That's a broad answer."

A small smile touched Imani's lips.

Marisol continued.

"You built this place from nothing."

Imani glanced around the office.

Nothing.

That wasn't entirely true.

She had started with a folding table.

An unreliable laptop.

And more determination than resources.

Back then nobody expected her to succeed.

Some openly expected her to fail.

Especially when she walked into rooms where nobody looked like her.

Nobody sounded like her.

Nobody believed she belonged.

She remembered every one of those rooms.

Every dismissal.

Every doubt.

Every person who mistook confidence for arrogance because it came from a woman.

"I remember sleeping in the office," she said quietly.

Marisol smiled.

"I remember."

"Seventy-hour weeks."

"Eighty."

Imani nodded.

"Eighty."

A brief silence settled.

Then came the part she rarely acknowledged.

Missed birthdays.

Missed vacations.

Missed anniversaries.

Missed family dinners.

Missed opportunities to simply live.

The company grew.

The sacrifices grew with it.

People called her driven.

Focused.

Exceptional.

Few ever asked what those achievements cost.

Fewer still wanted the honest answer.

Marisol studied her carefully.

"Was it worth it?"

Imani looked toward the city.

The question should have been easy.

Instead—

it wasn't.

"Most days," she said.

Marisol noticed the hesitation.

"Most days?"

Imani nodded.

People called her successful.

Nobody called her happy.

And lately—

she wasn't sure that distinction was small.

CHAPTER 8

Momentum didn't always announce itself.

It didn't arrive with noise or disruption.

Sometimes it showed up in the absence of resistance—in the way things

moved without friction.

By the end of the week, Malik wasn't being watched the same way.

At first, people had measured him.

Observed quietly.

Waited for something to reveal itself.

A misstep.

A hesitation.

A moment where the gap showed.

It hadn't come.

And now—

they were starting to move with him instead of around him.

Imani noticed the shift before anyone said it.

She always did.

At 9:14, she stepped into a meeting already in progress.

Conversations paused—briefly.

Not because they needed direction.

Because they registered her presence.

That part hadn't changed.

What had changed—

was what happened after.

They didn't immediately look to her.

They continued.

Imani remained near the entrance for a moment longer than usual,

observing.

Not interfering.

Because this—

this mattered.

Malik stood near the far end of the table.

Listening.

He didn't interrupt.

Didn't reposition himself to take command.

He let the conversation breathe.

Then—

"Let's pull this back."

The room shifted.

Not dramatically.

Subtly.

Because his tone didn't demand attention.

It assumed it.

Imani didn't move.

She wanted to see what happened when she didn't step in.

Malik redirected the conversation without overexplaining.

He removed the noise.

Focused the outcome.

And then—

he stepped back.

Didn't hold the floor.

Didn't linger in command.

That—

that was the difference.

Most people held onto authority once they established it.

He didn't.

Imani felt something settle.

Not approval.

Confirmation.

Later, when their paths crossed in the hallway, neither of them slowed.

Just a brief glance.

Recognition.

And then movement.

But internally—

Imani adjusted her assessment.

He wasn't adapting anymore.

He was influencing.

CHAPTER 9

Imani didn't draw conclusions quickly.

But she didn't ignore patterns either.

And Malik was becoming one.

Not predictable.

Consistent.

At 11:36, she called him in.

No explanation.

No context.

"Come to my office."

He arrived exactly when expected.

Not early.

Not late.

On time.

He didn't sit immediately.

Imani noticed.

"You can sit."

He did.

Not rushed.

Not hesitant.

Just deliberate.

Silence settled between them.

Imani let it remain.

Because she wanted to see if he would fill it.

He didn't.

"You're settling in quickly," she said.

Malik leaned back slightly.

"I'm doing the job."

Not deflection.

Not dismissal.

Just a fact.

"That's not the same thing," she said.

A brief pause.

"Then what do you see?" He asked.

That—

shifted the dynamic.

Imani started to respond —
then paused.

Not because she didn't know what to say.

But because, for once, she wanted to see what would happen
if she didn't take control immediately.

Imani leaned forward slightly.

"I see someone who doesn't need constant direction."

A beat.

"And doesn't create noise to prove value."

Malik held her gaze.

"That usually works better."

A slight shift in her expression.

"You'd be surprised how many people don't understand that."

Silence.

Then—

"You're also not asking questions you should be asking."

That changed the tone.

Malik didn't react immediately.

"What kind of questions?" he asked.

Imani didn't answer right away.

"The kind that define how far you can go here."

The words landed clean.

Malik leaned forward slightly.

"And if I already know that?"

There it was.

Imani held his gaze.

"Then you're either very aware…"

A pause.

"Or very confident."

Malik didn't look away.

"Which one do you think it is?"

Imani didn't answer.

Not yet.

"Time will answer that," she said.

Malik nodded.

"Fair."

As he stood to leave, he paused.

"You don't miss much," he said.

Imani's response came easily.

"No."

He held her gaze for a second longer—

then left.

And for the first time—

she acknowledged it.

He was different.

And that—

was starting to matter.

CHAPTER 10

That night, the shift became real.

Not in the office.

Outside of it.

The lounge sat tucked between glass buildings and city lights, carrying the kind of atmosphere that didn't need to announce itself.

Low music.

Muted conversations.

Warm lighting.

The kind of place people came when they wanted company without obligation.

Imani rarely came here.

Not because she disliked places like this.

Because she rarely made time for them.

Tonight felt different.

The moment she stepped inside, she saw him.

Malik sat at the far end of the bar.

Not scrolling through his phone.

Not engaged in conversation.

Just present.

Aware.

He noticed her immediately.

No surprise.

No performance.

Just acknowledgment.

Imani crossed the room and slid into the seat beside him.

"You don't seem surprised."

Malik glanced over.

"I'm not."

"You expected me?"

"No."

He lifted his glass.

"But I'm not surprised you're here."

Imani studied him.

"And why is that?"

A slight smile touched the corner of his mouth.

"Because people don't change their routines unless something is changing inside them."

That answer landed harder than she expected.

The bartender approached.

"What can I get you?"

Imani glanced at the menu.

Then looked away.

"Old Fashioned."

Malik nodded approvingly.

"Interesting choice."

She raised an eyebrow.

"Why?"

"You don't strike me as someone who orders sweet drinks."

That earned the smallest laugh.

"You've known me for a few weeks."

"Long enough."

The bartender returned with their drinks.

Silence settled.

Comfortable.

Not forced.

For the first time all week, Imani wasn't thinking about work.

The realization caught her off guard.

"What?"

Malik asked.

She looked at him.

"What do you mean?"

"You just realized something."

Imani stared into her glass.

"You always notice that?"

"Usually."

That answer should have annoyed her.

Instead—

it made her smile.

The conversation moved naturally after that.

Not strategically.

Not professionally.

Naturally.

They talked about childhood.

About growing up.

About ambition.

About expectations.

For the first time, Malik learned that Imani had always been the responsible one.

The one people depended on.

The one who solved problems.

The one who carried weight without complaining.

"And who took care of you?" he asked.

Imani paused.

Long enough to answer the question without speaking.

Malik nodded.

"That's what I thought."

For a moment neither spoke.

Then Imani asked,

"What about you?"

Malik leaned back.

"My grandmother."

The answer came easily.

"She raised me."

A smile crossed his face.

"She used to say that people tell you who they are every day. The problem is most people are too busy talking to notice."

Imani laughed softly.

"I like her already."

"You would've intimidated her."

That earned a genuine laugh.

"No."

"Absolutely."

The smile remained between them.

The conversation deepened.

Not dramatically.

Gradually.

The way meaningful conversations often do.

Dreams.

Failures.

Regrets.

Choices.

The things people rarely discussed in boardrooms.

At one point Malik studied her quietly.

"What?"

Imani asked.

"You know what's interesting?"

She waited.

"You spend all day taking care of problems."

A pause.

"But I don't think you know what to do when nobody needs you."

The words hit harder than anything else that evening.

Because she didn't have an answer.

Not immediately.

Not honestly.

For years her identity had been built around being needed.

Being valuable.

Being capable.

Who was she without that?

The question lingered.

And for the first time—

she didn't rush to answer it.

She simply sat with it.

Present.

Human.

Seen.

And surprisingly—

comfortable.

The evening continued.

Neither watching the clock.

Neither trying to end it.

Neither trying to define it.

For once—

the moment was enough.

CHAPTER 11

The next morning, everything returned to structure.

Schedules aligned.

Meetings moved.

Expectations remained.

Imani stepped into her office already focused.

No hesitation.

No distraction.

But something had followed her from the night before.

Not distraction.

Something quieter.

Something she hadn't made space for before.

Not emotion.

Awareness.

She noticed it in small ways.

A slight delay before responding.

A longer pause before making a decision.

Nothing obvious.

But enough.

The outcome was the same.

But it didn't feel the same.

And that difference — mattered.

At 10:26, Marisol stepped in.

"You look… different."

Imani didn't look up right away.

"Define different."

Marisol leaned lightly against the doorframe.

"Less contained."

That made Imani pause.

Because that—

wasn't something she heard often.

"Is that a problem?" she asked.

Marisol shook her head.

"No."

A small pause.

"Just noticeable."

Imani nodded once.

Then returned to her work.

But the observation stayed.

Because it wasn't inaccurate.

It was just—

new.

CHAPTER 12

Imani's apartment felt exactly the same.

And that was the problem.

Everything was where she left it—

clean lines, neutral tones, nothing out of place.

Nothing lived in.

She set her bag down in the same spot she always did.

Keys in the tray. Shoes aligned. Jacket hung.

Routine.

Control.

Predictable.

She walked further inside, slower this time, her heels quieter against the floor

than usual.

There was no noise here.

No friction.

No resistance.

No interruption.

Just... silence.

Imani stood in the middle of the room, her eyes moving across the space like

she was seeing it for the first time.

Not assessing.

Not adjusting.

Just… noticing.

That was the shift.

She wasn't managing the moment.

She was inside it.

And something about it felt off.

Not wrong.

Just…quieter than it should have been.

She exhaled slowly, setting her phone down without checking it.

That alone was new.

Normally, she would already be reviewing tomorrow.

Repositioning. Preparing.

Moving.

But tonight—

she didn't.

Instead, she walked to the window and looked out over the city.

Same skyline.

Same movement.

Same rhythm.

But she didn't feel separate from it the way she used to.

She felt… in it.

Connected to something she hadn't allowed herself to touch before.

Imani folded her arms lightly, her reflection faint against the glass.

For the first time in a long time—

she wasn't thinking about what needed to be controlled.

She was thinking about what she had been holding back.

And for the first time—

She wasn't sure if she wanted to tighten her grip…

Or finally let it go.

CHAPTER 13

By midweek, the shift wasn't just internal.

It was external.

People responded differently.

Not in authority.

That hadn't changed.

In energy.

Conversations moved more smoothly.

Less resistance.

Less friction.

Imani noticed it immediately.

Because she noticed everything.

It wasn't that she had softened.

She hadn't.

But something in her presence had adjusted.

And people responded to it.

At 2:11, Malik noticed it too.

"You're not pushing as hard."

Imani looked at him.

"I don't need to."

A brief pause.

"That's new," he said.

"It's different," she corrected.

Not defensive.

Just...aware.

She didn't deny it.

"Yes."

Silence followed.

But it didn't feel uncertain.

It felt… understood.

CHAPTER 14

"You're not answering your phone the same way."

Imani looked up from her glass, her expression neutral.

"What does that mean?"

Marisol didn't respond immediately. She rarely did when she was choosing

her words carefully.

"It means," she said finally, "you pause now."

A small silence settled between them.

Imani leaned back slightly. "I've always paused."

Marisol shook her head.

"No," she said. "You calculated."

That landed.

Not as criticism.

As clarity.

"You moved like every second already belonged to something," Marisol

continued. "Like there was no space for anything unexpected."

Imani didn't interrupt.

Didn't correct it.

Because she knew—

that was true.

"And now?" Imani asked.

Marisol studied her for a moment longer than usual.

"Now it feels like you're deciding what deserves your time… instead of

assuming everything does."

Imani held her gaze.

That wasn't a small shift.

That was identity.

"And that's a problem?" she asked.

Marisol's expression softened slightly.

"No," she said.

A beat.

"It's just… different."

CHAPTER 15

Imani didn't define things too early.

She let them develop.

Take shape before assigning meaning.

But this—

was becoming harder to ignore.

At 6:08, she stepped into the lounge again.

Not out of habit.

Choice.

Malik was already there.

He didn't look surprised this time.

"You're becoming predictable," he said.

Imani raised an eyebrow.

"I don't do predictable."

A faint smile crossed his face.

"Then call it consistent."

That—

felt more accurate.

She took the seat beside him without hesitation.

And this time—

the space between them felt different.

Not undefined.

Developing.

And that shift —

Carried more weight than either of them acknowledged out loud.

"You're not avoiding this," he said.

Imani met his gaze.

"No."

A brief pause.

"Are you?"

Malik didn't look away.

"No."

Silence settled.

But this time—

it wasn't measured.

It was mutual.

And just like that—

the line between them became clear.

Not spoken.

But understood.

CHAPTER 16

The restaurant wasn't expensive.

That was the first thing Imani noticed.

Not because she cared about cost.

Because she expected something different.

Malik noticed her observation immediately.

"You expected white tablecloths."

"I expected something."

A smile crossed his face.

"This is something."

The place was small.

Local.

Comfortable.

The kind of restaurant people returned to because of consistency rather than status.

And somehow—

that felt appropriate.

Dinner started easily.

No discussion of projects.

No meetings.

No strategy.

Just conversation.

The kind that existed when people genuinely wanted to know each other.

They talked about family traditions.

Favorite meals.

Holiday memories.

Embarrassing childhood stories.

Imani couldn't remember the last time she laughed this much.

Not politely.

Actually laughed.

The kind that left her shoulders relaxed.

The kind that made time disappear.

At one point Malik leaned back and looked at her.

"You know what I think?"

Imani raised an eyebrow.

"That sounds dangerous."

"It probably is."

She smiled.

"I think you've spent so much time building your future that you forgot you're allowed to enjoy your present."

The statement settled between them.

Not uncomfortable.

Accurate.

Imani stared down at her glass.

For years every decision had been connected to the next goal.

The next milestone.

The next achievement.

The next level.

Always moving.

Always building.

Always preparing.

Rarely arriving.

And yet—

sitting here—

she felt something she hadn't felt in a long time.

Content.

Not because everything was perfect.

Because she wasn't trying to improve the moment.

She was experiencing it.

The distinction mattered.

The evening stretched longer than planned.

Neither seemed eager to leave.

Outside, the city lights reflected across the sidewalk.

The air felt lighter.

Softer.

For a moment they simply stood there.

Neither rushing.

Neither forcing.

Just present.

Imani looked at him.

For the first time—

she wasn't evaluating the future.

She was imagining one.

And that realization changed everything.

CHAPTER 17

Imani didn't rush into anything.

Not decisions.

Not people.

Not moments she hadn't fully understood yet.

Everything in her life had structure because she made sure it did.

But recently—

structure felt… less rigid.

Not gone.

Adjusted.

At 8:18, she noticed it in the smallest way.

She didn't reach for her schedule immediately.

Instead, she stood in her kitchen a moment longer than usual, coffee in hand,

watching the city move into its day.

No urgency.

No immediate shift into motion.

That alone—

was a change.

And she knew exactly where it came from.

Not distraction.

Awareness.

And awareness—

once it settled—

didn't leave easily.

CHAPTER 18

Malik didn't chase.

That was one of the first things Imani understood about him.

He didn't create moments.

Didn't push for time.

Didn't lean into proximity just because it was available.

He let things happen.

At first, she interpreted that as distance.

Now—

she saw it differently.

It wasn't distance.

It was structure.

A different kind than hers.

Less structured.

But just as deliberate.

At 6:32, she tested it.

Not obviously.

But intentionally.

She delayed responding to a message she normally would have answered

immediately.

Left space.

Waited.

There was no follow-up.

No second message.

No adjustment.

He didn't fill the gap.

He respected it.

And that—

that told her more than anything else could have.

CHAPTER 19

By the end of the week, the shift wasn't subtle anymore.

It wasn't just conversation.

It was presence.

They moved around each other differently.

Not carefully.

Aware.

At 6:03, the line changed.

Not spoken.

Felt.

"You don't keep things casual," Malik said.

Imani met his gaze.

"No."

A brief pause.

"And you?"

Malik didn't hesitate.

"I don't build things halfway."

The words settled between them —

not heavy.

Just...certain.

The words weren't emphasized.

They didn't need to be.

Because what sat underneath them—

was clear.

This wasn't something either of them was approaching lightly.

And that—

made it real.

CHAPTER 20

Imani didn't lose control.

She adjusted it.

There was a difference.

At 9:11, she let someone finish a thought she normally would have

redirected.

At 11:47, she didn't correct something immediately.

At 2:26, she paused instead of deciding.

Each moment—

intentional.

Because she was learning something she hadn't needed before.

Control didn't always require holding everything in place.

Sometimes—

it required knowing when to step back.

That wasn't instinct.

It was choice.

And she was making it more often.

CHAPTER 21

That night, the shift became undeniable.

Not in conversation.

In proximity.

They stood closer than usual.

Not by accident.

Not addressed.

Imani felt it immediately.

Not as tension.

As awareness.

The kind that didn't require explanation.

This wasn't just building anymore.

It was becoming something.

And for the first time—

she didn't try to define it.

Didn't step back.

Didn't redirect.

She let it exist.

Fully.

Because now—

it wasn't unclear.

It was just—

unspoken.

And sometimes—

that carried more weight than anything else.

CHAPTER 22

Imani didn't avoid difficult conversations.

She delayed them sometimes—

not out of hesitation,

but precision.

Timing mattered.

Context mattered.

Clarity mattered.

But this—

this wasn't something that could stay unspoken much longer.

It had moved past observation.

Past awareness.

Into something that required definition.

At 6:14, she didn't wait for the moment to present itself.

She created it.

"We need to define this."

Malik didn't look surprised.

If anything—

he looked like he had been waiting for it.

"Do we?" he asked.

Not dismissive.

Just...certain she was already closer to an answer than she was admitting.

Imani held his gaze.

"Yes."

A pause.

"Because I don't move without clarity."

Malik leaned back slightly, studying her in a way that wasn't confrontational.

"And you think this doesn't have it?"

There it was.

Not resistance.

Challenge.

Imani exhaled slowly.

"It has direction."

A brief pause.

"Not definition."

Silence settled between them.

But it didn't feel unresolved.

It felt—

necessary.

Something that had been building—

finally acknowledged.

CHAPTER 23

Malik didn't rush his response.

He never did.

"That depends on what you need it to be," he said.

Imani didn't look away.

"I don't need anything undefined."

A slight shift in his posture.

Not defensive.

Engaged.

"Then define it," he said.

That landed differently than she expected.

Not as pressure.

As responsibility.

Imani held his gaze a second longer.

Because now—

this wasn't about interpretation.

It was about choice.

"This isn't casual," she said.

Malik nodded once.

"I know."

A pause.

"And it doesn't stay separate from everything else."

Another nod.

"I know that too."

Silence settled again.

But this time—

it wasn't uncertain.

It was alignment—

waiting to be confirmed.

CHAPTER 24

Imani didn't hesitate often.

But when she did—

it meant something.

"This affects how I move," she said.

Her voice stayed even.

But there was weight behind it now.

"Everything I do has impact."

Malik didn't interrupt.

Didn't soften it.

Didn't minimize it.

"I'm aware," he said.

Imani studied him.

"And you're still here."

A brief pause.

"Yes."

No explanation.

No elaboration.

Just certainty.

And for the first time—

she didn't question it.

She accepted it.

CHAPTER 25

The shift didn't happen dramatically.

There was no moment that marked it.

No declaration.

No visible line crossed.

Just—

Decision.

At 7:02, they didn't step away.

At 7:03, they didn't create distance.

At 7:04—

they stayed exactly where they were.

And that—

that was the answer.

Not spoken.

Chosen.

Imani felt it settle.

Not as pressure.

As clarity.

This wasn't something she was evaluating anymore.

It was something she was in.

Fully.

CHAPTER 26

By noon, the issue had spread beyond the original team.

That was the problem with visibility.

Success attracted attention.

Mistakes attracted scrutiny.

Imani sat at the head of the conference table, reviewing the preliminary findings for a third time.

The discrepancy wasn't catastrophic.

But it wasn't insignificant either.

More importantly—

it was visible.

And visibility changed everything.

The door opened.

Three senior executives entered.

None of them were part of the original review process.

That told her everything she needed to know.

The situation had grown.

"We need to discuss exposure," one of them said.

Imani remained calm.

"We need to discuss facts."

The executive took a seat.

"Perception becomes fact if we allow it."

There it was.

The real problem.

Not the discrepancy.

The narrative.

Imani folded her hands.

"Then we'll control the narrative with transparency."

A silence followed.

Not everyone agreed.

She could see it.

Some wanted distance.

Some wanted blame.

Some wanted protection.

Few wanted accountability.

And accountability was exactly where she intended to start.

As the meeting continued, Imani noticed something else.

People weren't simply evaluating the situation.

They were evaluating her.

Watching.

Measuring.

Waiting to see whether the pressure changed her decisions.

It wouldn't.

But that didn't mean she ignored the risk.

Because for the first time in years—

the room felt political.

And politics rarely cared about truth.

CHAPTER 27

The external review began the following morning.

Two auditors.

Three compliance specialists.

One representative from oversight.

Five people whose only job was to find what everyone else missed.

Imani welcomed them personally.

Not because she had to.

Because leadership became visible during difficult moments.

The first question came immediately.

"How long has this issue existed?"

Direct.

Expected.

Imani answered without hesitation.

"We're still determining that."

The auditor nodded.

Writing.

Watching.

Evaluating.

For the next four hours, every process was examined.

Every decision questioned.

Every assumption challenged.

By lunch, the atmosphere had changed.

Not hostile.

Clinical.

And clinical environments rarely offered grace.

Late that afternoon, Malik stepped into her office.

"You haven't eaten."

"I'm aware."

He closed the door.

"That's not what I said."

Imani leaned back.

For a moment, she considered pushing the comment aside.

Instead—

she smiled.

Slightly.

"You always do that."

"Do what?"

"Say one thing while meaning another."

Malik folded his arms.

"No."

A pause.

"I say exactly what I mean."

For the first time that day—

she laughed.

The tension eased.

Only briefly.

But it mattered.

Because outside the office door, everyone was questioning the situation.

Inside—

someone was reminding her she wasn't carrying it alone.

CHAPTER 28

The rumor started before the facts were finished.

Imani should have expected that.

Information moved quickly.

Speculation moved faster.

By mid-afternoon, she noticed conversations stopping when she entered rooms.

Not dramatically.

Subtly.

Enough to register.

Enough to matter.

Marisol noticed it too.

"They don't know anything."

Imani looked up.

"No."

A pause.

"They think they do."

The distinction mattered.

People filled gaps with assumptions.

Always had.

Always would.

Marisol sat across from her desk.

"You worried?"

Imani considered the question.

Not about the review.

Not about the findings.

About trust.

Trust took years to build.

Minutes to damage.

And almost impossible effort to restore.

"A little."

Marisol smiled.

The answer surprised her.

"That sounded honest."

Imani smiled slightly.

"Don't get used to it."

Both women laughed.

But beneath the laughter sat a truth neither ignored.

This situation wasn't testing procedures.

It was testing leadership.

And leadership became most visible when people started doubting.

CHAPTER 29

The recommendation arrived on Thursday.

Imani read it twice.

Then a third time.

Not because it was confusing.

Because it carried consequences.

Additional oversight.

Temporary restrictions.

Enhanced reporting requirements.

Nothing permanent.

Nothing devastating.

But enough to create questions.

Enough to create headlines.

Enough to create doubt.

The board meeting that followed lasted three hours.

Three long hours of explanations.

Challenges.

Clarifications.

By the end, one director asked the question everyone else avoided.

"Can you still lead this organization objectively?"

Silence filled the room.

Imani held his gaze.

The question wasn't offensive.

It was necessary.

Which made it more important.

"Yes."

The answer came immediately.

Not defensive.

Certain.

The director nodded.

But she understood something in that moment.

Leadership wasn't proven when everyone trusted you.

Leadership was proven when trust became optional.

And despite everything—

she remained standing.

Remained clear.

Remained herself.

That mattered.

More than any report ever could.

CHAPTER 30

The package arrived on Friday.

No return address.

No company markings.

No explanation.

Imani almost ignored it.

Almost.

Something about it felt intentional.

She opened it carefully.

Inside sat a single photograph.

Nothing else.

At first glance, it appeared ordinary.

Then she looked closer.

The image showed her.

Not recently.

Months ago.

Leaving a meeting.

Crossing a parking garage.

Completely unaware she was being photographed.

A second photograph sat underneath.

Another location.

Another day.

Another moment.

Her stomach tightened.

Not fear.

Recognition.

Someone had been watching.

Systematically.

Deliberately.

The final item in the package was a folded sheet of paper.

One sentence.

Typed.

No signature.

No explanation.

No demand.

Just words.

"You've become visible."

Imani read the sentence again.

Then once more.

Not shaken.

Not uncertain.

Aware.

Because visibility came with consequences.

And whoever sent this wanted her to understand that.

She looked out across the city.

The same skyline.

The same movement.

The same world.

Yet suddenly—

it felt different.

The package wasn't a warning.

It was proof.

She was already inside the game.

Imani placed the photographs back inside the box.

Carefully.

Deliberately.

The way people handled something dangerous when they weren't ready to call it a threat.

She looked at the images again.

Different days.

Different locations.

Different angles.

Not random.

Pattern.

Someone had invested time.

That mattered.

Her phone sat on the desk.

For the first time in years, she considered calling someone before solving the problem herself.

The thought surprised her.

Not because she needed help.

Because she trusted someone enough to share the weight.

Her thumb hovered over Malik's name.

Then stopped.

Not yet.

First she needed facts.

But the realization remained.

She no longer carried everything alone.

And that changed the way the photographs felt.

Not less serious.

Less isolating.

CHAPTER 31

By the next morning, everything had changed.

And nothing had.

Imani still moved the same way.

Still led with precision.

Still maintained control.

But internally—

something had shifted.

She wasn't holding distance anymore.

Not from him.

Not from what this had become.

At 9:36, their paths crossed in the office.

No pause.

No adjustment.

Just—

recognition.

A brief exchange of eye contact that didn't need explanation.

And then movement.

But that moment—

small as it was—

carried more weight than anything that had been said.

Because now—

this wasn't undefined.

It wasn't labeled.

But it wasn't uncertain either.

It was understood.

And that understanding—

changed how everything moved from that point forward.

Yet beneath that understanding sat something else.

The package.

The photographs.

The sentence she couldn't stop replaying.

You've become visible.

Imani had spent years building influence.

She understood visibility.

But this felt different.

Personal.

Targeted.

Intentional.

For the first time in a long time—

she wasn't just thinking about what she was building.

She was thinking about who might want to take it away.

CHAPTER 32

Nothing about Monday looked different.

Same schedule.

Same structure.

Same expectations.

But Imani felt the shift the moment she stepped into the building.

Not because anything had changed around her.

Because something had changed in how she moved through it.

There was no separation anymore.

No version of herself she stepped into once she crossed the threshold into

work.

Everything—

was aligned.

And alignment—

carried weight.

At 8:52, she moved through her first meeting without interruption.

Not because there was nothing to correct.

Because she chose not to correct it.

That choice—

was new.

Not lack of control.

Refinement of it.

CHAPTER 33

Space showed up in places she hadn't allowed it before.

Not in her schedule.

In her decisions.

Imani didn't fill every silence anymore.

Didn't immediately tighten control when something shifted slightly off track.

At 11:18, she let a conversation run longer than it needed to.

Not because she lost focus.

Because she wanted to see what would happen without her intervention.

The room adjusted.

People corrected themselves.

Found clarity without her direction.

That—

was new.

And it worked.

But with that shift—

came something else.

Visibility.

CHAPTER 34

The first sign of pressure came quietly.

An email.

Marked urgent.

Imani read it once.

Then again.

There was a discrepancy.

Not large.

But noticeable.

And in her position—

noticeable was enough.

At 10:02, she walked into the meeting already clear on what mattered.

Not the mistake.

The response.

Because mistakes happened.

What mattered now —

was how she moved when everything was visible.

What defined leadership—

was how they were handled.

She didn't sit immediately.

Didn't open the conversation.

She let someone else start.

Listened.

Watched.

And measured.

CHAPTER 35

The room felt different before anything was said.

More people.

More attention.

Less margin for error.

"This isn't just internal," someone said.

Imani didn't react.

She already knew.

"This triggers external review."

There it was.

Not escalation.

Exposure.

And exposure—

changed everything.

Imani leaned back slightly.

"Then we stay ahead of it."

Not defensive.

Not reactive.

Decisive.

But this time—

it wasn't just about process.

It was about perception.

And perception—

spread faster than facts.

And once it moved —

it didn't ask for permission to define the narrative.

CHAPTER 36

The review didn't disrupt the structure.

It tightened it.

Processes sharpened.

Conversations became more direct.

Expectations clearer.

At 11:06, the first real question surfaced.

"How closely are you working with Malik on this?"

The room didn't move.

But attention shifted.

Imani didn't hesitate.

"Directly."

A brief pause.

"And outside of that?"

The question wasn't about process.

It was about perception.

And everyone in the room knew it.

There it was.

The question behind the question.

Imani held their gaze.

"It doesn't affect outcomes."

She didn't elaborate.

Didn't clarify.

She defined it.

And let it stand.

The silence that followed wasn't uncertain.

It was measured.

Because now—

they weren't just evaluating the situation.

They were evaluating her.

And for the first time—

she understood how quickly perception could become leverage.

The relationship itself wasn't the issue.

The assumption of influence was.

That distinction mattered.

Because leadership wasn't judged solely by decisions.

It was judged by what people believed shaped them.

And belief—

was harder to control than facts.

And Imani—

never moved without knowing exactly what that meant.

CHAPTER 37

Pressure didn't break Imani.

It clarified her.

But this time—

it wasn't just external.

At 2:18, the shift became direct.

Not about the situation.

About her.

"Would you have made the same decision without his input?"

The question wasn't aggressive.

But it was intentional.

The room didn't move.

But the air changed.

Imani didn't respond immediately.

Not because she needed time to think.

Because the question required precision.

"Yes," she said.

A brief pause.

"And I would make it again."

Her tone didn't shift.

Didn't harden.

Didn't soften.

It stayed exactly where it needed to be.

The answer stood on its own.

But later—

alone—

she revisited it.

Not with doubt.

With clarity.

Because now—

every decision carried more weight than it had before.

And she felt it.

Not as pressure.

As awareness.

CHAPTER 38

Resolution didn't arrive as relief.

It arrived as direction.

By Thursday, the findings were clear.

There were gaps.

But nothing broken.

The structure held.

That mattered more than anything else.

Imani read the report without reaction.

Not because it didn't matter.

Because it confirmed what she already understood.

At 10:44, she closed the file.

And for the first time in days—

she paused.

Not because she needed to recover.

Because she could.

That distinction—

mattered.

Because she hadn't lost control.

She had maintained it.

Under pressure.

Under scrutiny.

And that—

was the real measure.

But as she gathered the report and prepared for the next meeting, another realization surfaced.

The review had ended.

The attention hadn't.

People were still watching.

Still measuring.

Still deciding what her success meant to them.

The package had proven that.

The review had confirmed it.

Visibility wasn't temporary anymore.

It was permanent.

CHAPTER 39

The future wasn't something Imani feared.

It was something she built.

Deliberately.

But now—

it wasn't just hers.

That realization didn't arrive dramatically.

It settled.

Standing at the overlook, the city stretched out in front of her.

Malik stood beside her.

Not speaking.

Not interrupting the moment.

Just present.

"This doesn't stay small," she said.

Malik nodded.

"It's not supposed to."

She turned slightly toward him.

"And you're ready for that?"

He didn't hesitate.

"Yes."

That answer didn't feel heavy.

It felt… certain.

And certainty—

when it matched her own—

didn't create tension.

It created alignment.

And for the first time—

she didn't feel like she was carrying the future alone.

CHAPTER 40

The outside world noticed.

It always did.

But this time—

the response was immediate.

Opportunities appeared quickly.

Too quickly.

Emails.

Calls.

Requests for alignment.

Imani didn't respond right away.

Because attention—

wasn't the same as value.

At 2:09, one message stood out.

Not because of who sent it.

Because of what it implied.

They weren't asking to collaborate.

They were asking for access.

That—

changed everything.

Access meant visibility.

Visibility meant influence.

And influence—

when not controlled—

shifted power.

Imani leaned back slightly.

Reading it again.

Not reacting.

Assessing.

Because this wasn't an opportunity.

It was a test.

CHAPTER 41

The offer was clear.

Too clear.

Shared oversight.

Expanded reach.

Protection.

And in return—

influence.

Control.

Imani didn't need time to consider it.

She already understood what it meant.

"I'm not handing over what I built," she said.

Her tone didn't rise.

Didn't shift.

It stayed controlled.

Definitive.

Malik didn't respond immediately.

Then—

"Then don't."

Simple.

Direct.

But it mattered.

Because it wasn't advice.

It wasn't influence.

It was alignment.

He wasn't telling her what to do.

He was confirming what she had already decided.

And that—

that reinforced everything.

Because now—

she wasn't navigating this alone.

She was choosing it.

Fully.

CHAPTER 42

Imani didn't reject the offer.

She reframed it.

That distinction mattered.

Saying no would have ended the conversation.

What she did instead—

shifted it.

At 10:02, she sat across from them again.

Same room.

Same expectations.

Different position.

"I'm not interested in integration," she said.

No buildup.

No softening.

A brief pause.

"But I am open to strategic collaboration."

The words landed exactly where they needed to.

Not defensive.

Controlled.

"You're limiting our influence," one of them said.

Imani held his gaze.

"I'm protecting mine."

Silence followed.

Not uncomfortable.

Recalibrating.

Because now—

they weren't negotiating from leverage.

They were responding to it.

CHAPTER 43

The next level didn't arrive quietly.

It didn't need to.

Imani felt it in everything.

More visibility.

More expectation.

More weight behind every decision.

At 9:12, her calendar reflected it.

Meetings she hadn't been included in before.

Conversations that shaped direction—

not just execution.

She didn't react to it.

She stepped into it.

Because this—

this was where she belonged.

And she moved like it.

CHAPTER 44

Her phone lit up again.

Malik.

Imani looked at it longer than she needed to.

Not because she didn't want to answer.

Because she knew what answering meant.

Another step.

Another shift.

Another decision she wouldn't be able to walk back.

The screen dimmed.

Then lit again.

He wasn't rushing her.

Of course he wasn't.

Imani exhaled slowly and picked it up.

"Imani."

"You're still at the office."

Not a question.

She glanced around the room, then back toward the glass.

"Yes."

A brief pause.

"You don't have to be," he said.

Simple.

Direct.

And for the first time—

that wasn't something she dismissed.

"I know."

Silence settled between them.

Not empty.

Not uncertain.

Just… present.

Imani closed the file in front of her.

Not because it was done.

Because she was.

"I'm leaving," she said.

Another pause.

Then—

"Good."

Imani stood for a moment after the call ended.

Looking at the dark reflection in the office glass.

A few months ago she would have stayed.

Worked another hour.

Solved another problem.

Won another battle no one else knew existed.

Tonight—

she chose differently.

Not because the work mattered less.

Because she finally understood she mattered too.

She ended the call, reaching for her bag.

No hesitation this time.

No second-guessing.

Just movement.

And as she walked out of the office—

she didn't feel like she was stepping away from something important.

She felt like she was finally stepping into it.

CHAPTER 45

The cost showed up gradually.

Not in failure.

In time.

Longer days.

Fewer pauses.

Less separation between work and everything else.

At 6:18, she saw it clearly.

A missed call.

Malik.

She looked at the screen for a moment before setting the phone down.

Not ignoring it.

Still moving.

That—

that was the shift.

And when she finally stepped outside—

he was there.

Waiting.

"You're pushing too far," he said.

Imani met his gaze.

"I'm moving forward."

A brief pause.

"That's not the same thing."

The words didn't land as criticism.

They landed as truth.

And truth—

when it came from the right place—

wasn't something she dismissed.

CHAPTER 46

Imani didn't pull back.

She adjusted.

That was the difference.

At 7:06, she made the first change.

Not in her work.

In her boundaries.

She created space.

Not where it didn't matter.

Where it did.

Later that evening, she found him waiting again.

But this time—

it didn't feel like tension.

It felt… balanced.

"I heard you," she said.

Malik studied her for a moment.

Then nodded.

"I can tell."

And just like that—

the pressure shifted.

Not gone.

Aligned.

CHAPTER 47

The defining moment didn't arrive with intensity.

It never did.

It showed up in a decision.

At 3:32, the situation escalated again.

Unexpected.

The room filled quickly.

Questions surfaced.

Expectations followed.

"Who takes point on this?" Someone asked.

All eyes turned.

To her.

Imani felt it.

The assumption.

The expectation that she would step forward—

take control—

carry it.

She could have.

She always had.

But this time—

she didn't.

"Malik leads it."

The room went still.

Not in doubt.

In recognition.

"You're sure?" someone asked.

Imani didn't hesitate.

"Yes."

A brief pause.

"He has full authority."

The shift was immediate.

Focus moved.

Responsibility transferred.

And just like that—

the decision stood.

Later, in the hallway—

he stopped in front of her.

"You didn't take it," he said.

Imani met his gaze.

"I didn't need to."

A quiet pause settled between them.

"That's trust."

Imani held his gaze.

"That's alignment."

Not control.

Not distance.

Something stronger.

Something chosen.

Silence followed.

But it wasn't empty.

It was complete.

Because now—

nothing about this was uncertain.

Not the work.

Not the pressure.

Not them.

Everything held.

Or so it seemed.

Because while trust had settled into place—

something else was moving.

Quietly.

Beyond the walls of the organization.

Beyond the conversations.

Beyond anything they could currently see.

And when it finally arrived—

it wouldn't ask permission.

She hadn't lost control.

She had just learned —

she didn't need as much of it.

That night, Imani stood alone on the balcony.

The city stretched endlessly below.

Lights.

Movement.

Possibility.

Her phone buzzed.

One new message.

No name.

No number.

Just text.

She opened it.

Three words.

WE SEE YOU.

Nothing else.

No explanation.

No response option.

No mistake.

Imani stared at the screen.

Then slowly looked out across the city.

Somewhere—

someone was watching.

And for the first time—

she knew she wasn't imagining it.

The future was coming.

Faster than expected.

And it already knew her name.

END OF BOOK 1

AFTER 5: THE POWER SHIFT

The call didn't come through her assistant.

It came directly to her.

Imani looked at the screen for a moment longer than usual.

Unknown number.

She answered anyway.

"Imani."

A brief pause.

"We've been watching how you handled the last situation."

Her expression didn't change.

"Who is this?"

Silence.

"Someone with an opportunity you're not currently positioned to see."

Imani leaned back slightly.

"I don't engage in undefined conversations."

A quiet exhale.

"Then let me define it."

Another pause.

"What you've built—it's visible now."

Her gaze sharpened.

"And visibility at that level…"

A beat.

"changes who starts paying attention."

Imani didn't respond.

Because she already understood.

"This isn't about collaboration," the voice continued.

"It's about control."

There it was.

"What exactly are you offering?" she asked.

A pause.

"Access."

Another.

"Influence."

And then—

"Or protection… depending on how you choose to move."

The line went silent.

Imani lowered the phone slowly.

Not shaken.

Not uncertain.

But aware.

Because this—

was different.

This wasn't about alignment.

This was about power—

moving toward her.

Coming in Book 2